First American edition published in 2013 by Gecko Press USA, an imprint of Gecko Press Ltd.
A catalog record for this book is available from the US Library of Congress.

Distributed in the United States and Canada by Lerner Publishing Group, Inc.
241 First Avenue North, Minneapolis, MN 55401 USA
www.lernerbooks.com

This edition first published in 2013 by Gecko Press
PO Box 9335, Marion Square, Wellington 6141, New Zealand
info@geckopress.com

English language edition © Gecko Press Ltd 2013

Original title: C'est à moi, ça!
© 2009, l'école des loisirs, Paris
Text and illustrations by Michel Van Zeveren

A catalogue record for this book is available from the National Library of New Zealand.

Edited by Penelope Todd
Typesetting by Luke Kelly, New Zealand
Printed by Everbest, China

ISBN hardback: 978-1-877579-27-1
ISBN paperback: 978-1-877579-28-8

For more curiously good books, visit www.geckopress.com

MICHEL VAN ZEVEREN

That's Mine!

GECKO PRESS

In the jungle, the mighty jungle…

...a little frog finds an egg.

"Aha...
that's mine!"

"Hsss…

hsss…

hsss…

…sssmine,"

says the snake.

"Ack...

ack...

ack...

...actually, it's mine,"
says the eagle.

"Tut,

tut,

tut…

...'tis mine,"
says the lizard.

"No, mine!"
says the eagle.

"No, mine!"
says the lizard.

In the thick of the fight,
the egg takes off.

And lands…
on an elephant's head!

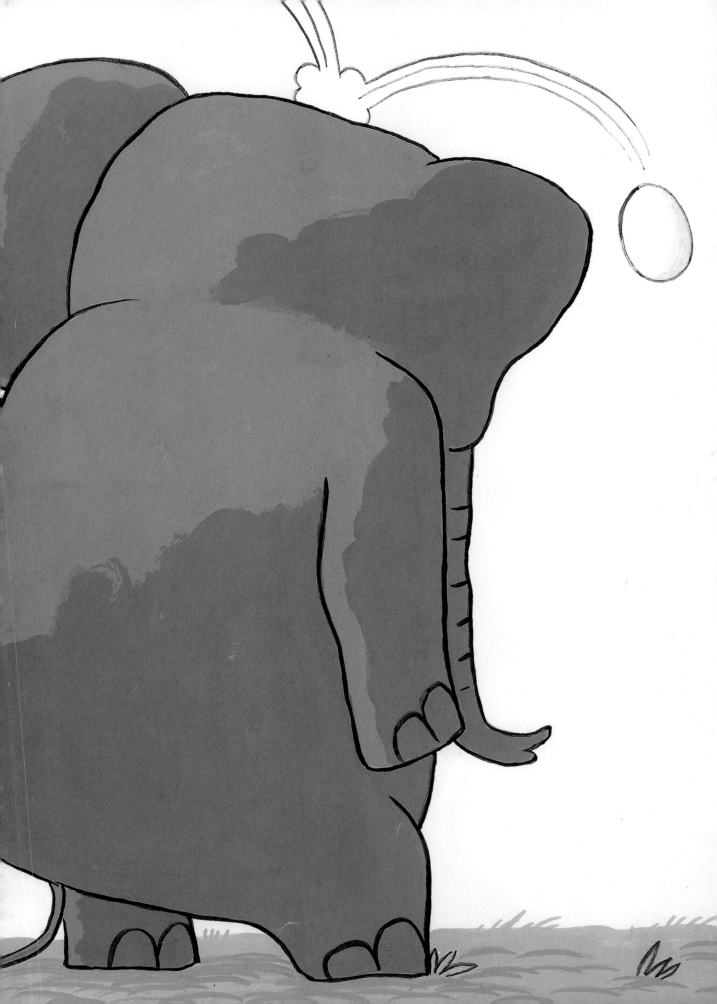

"Ouch!" says the elephant,

who now has a lump on his head.

"Well then, here you are,"
says the elephant.

"Aha!
I knew it
was mine!"
says the frog.

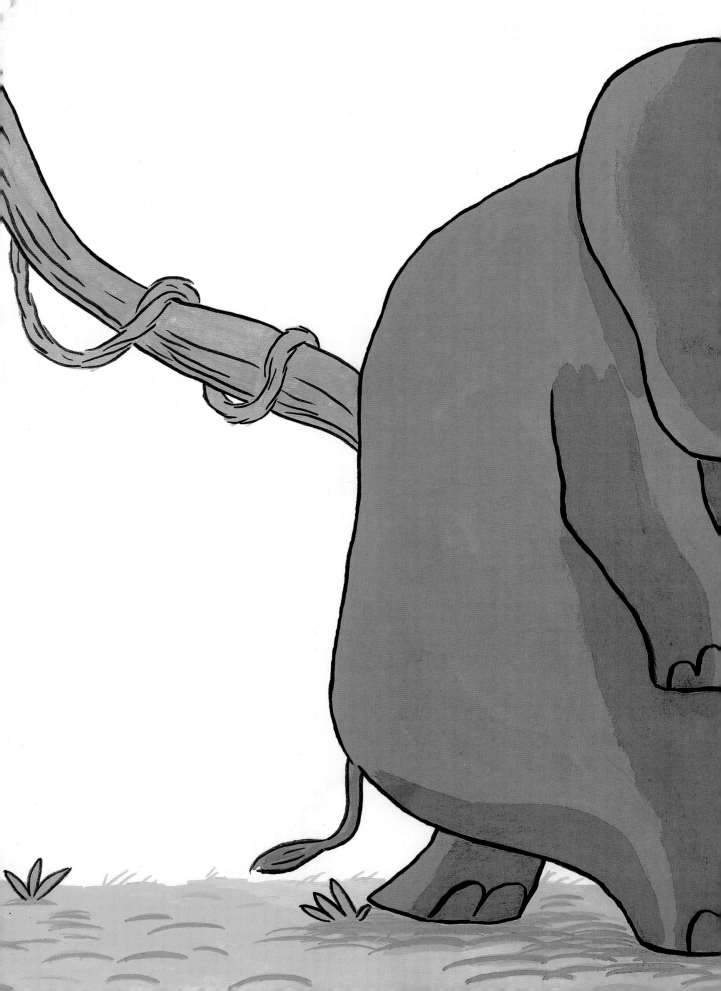

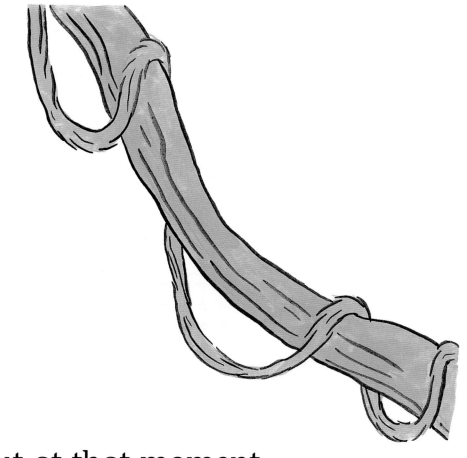

But at that moment,
the egg starts to crack.

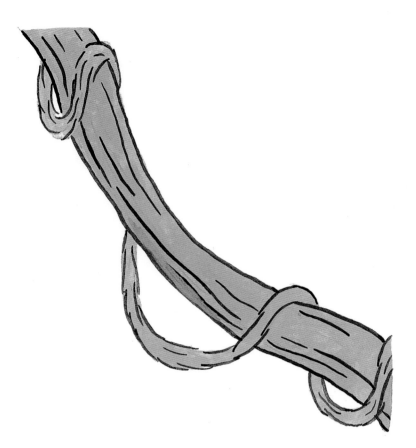

And out comes...
a crocodile!

She looks at the frog
and cries,

"Mine!"

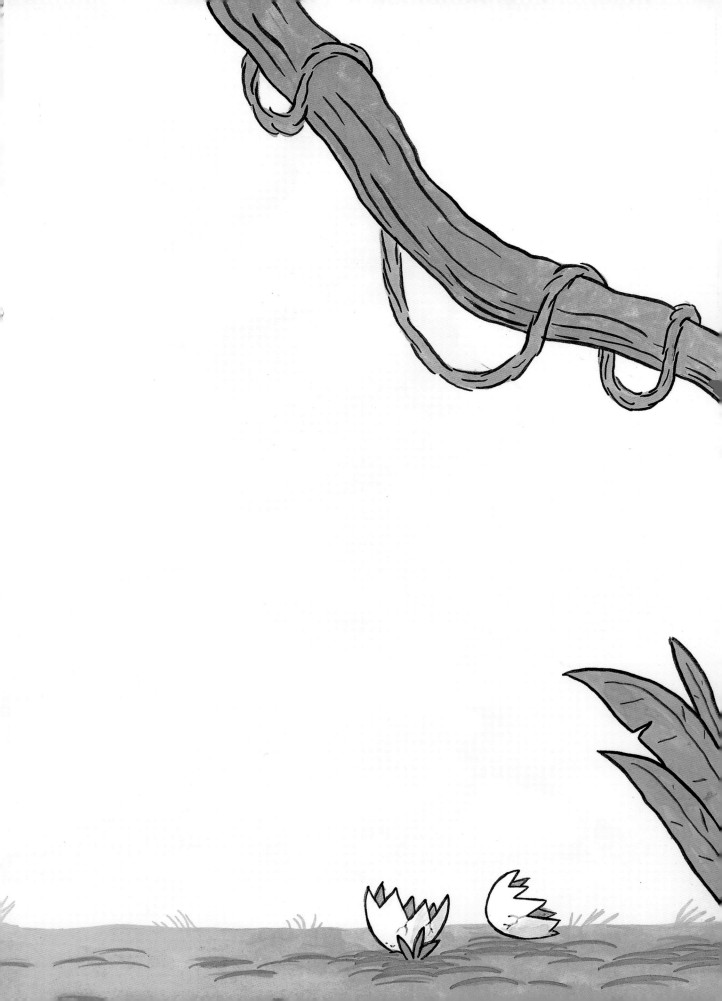